THE BUTCHER

Alina Reyes has published
two novels in France,
Le Boucher (*The Butcher*)
and *Lucie au Long Cours*,
also published by Methuen
in 1992.

ALINA REYES

The Butcher

*translated from the French
by David Watson*

Minerva

A Minerva Paperback
THE BUTCHER

First published in Great Britain 1991
by Methuen London
This Minerva edition published 1992
by Mandarin Paperbacks
Michelin House, 81 Fulham Road, London SW3 6RB

Minerva is an imprint of the Octopus Publishing Group,
a division of Reed International Books Limited

First published as *Le Boucher* in 1988
by Editions du Seuil

Copyright © 1988 by Alina Reyes
The author has asserted her moral rights
Translation copyright © 1991 by David Watson

A CIP catalogue record for this title
is available from the British Library
ISBN 0 7493 9984 8

Printed and bound in Great Britain
by Cox and Wyman Limited, Reading, Berks

THE BUTCHER

I

The blade plunged gently into the muscle then ran its full length in one supple movement. The action was perfectly controlled. The slice curled over limply onto the chopping block.

The black meat glistened, revived by the touch of the knife. The butcher placed his left hand flat on the broad rib and with his right hand began to carve into the thick meat once again. I could feel that cold elastic mass beneath the palm of my own hand. I saw the knife enter the firm dead flesh, opening it up like a shining wound. The steel blade slid down the length of the dark shape. The blade and the wall gleamed.

The butcher picked up the slices one after the other and placed them side by side on the chopping block. They fell with a flat slap – like a kiss against the wood.

With the point of the knife the butcher began to dress the meat, cutting out the yellow fat and splattering it against the tiled wall. He ripped a piece of greaseproof paper from the wad hanging on the iron hook, placed a slice in the middle of it, dropped another on top. The kiss again, more like a clap.

Then he turned to me, the heavy packet flat on his hand; he tossed it onto the scales.

The sickly smell of raw meat hit my nostrils. Seen close up, in the full summer morning light which poured in through the long window, it was bright red, beautifully nauseating. Who said that flesh is sad? Flesh is not sad, it is sinister. It belongs on the left side of our souls, it catches us at times of the greatest abandonment, carries us over deep seas, scuttles us and saves us; flesh is our guide, our dense black light, the well which draws our life down in a spiral, sucking it into oblivion.

The flesh of the bull before me was the same as that of the beast in the field, except that the blood had left it, the stream which carries life and carries it away so quickly, of which there remained only a few drops like pearls on the white paper.

And the butcher who talked to me about sex all day long was made of the same flesh, only warm, sometimes soft sometimes hard; the butcher had his good and inferior cuts, exacting and eager to burn out their life, to transform themselves into meat. And my flesh was the same, I who felt the fire light between my legs at the butcher's words.

There was a slit along the bottom of the butcher's stall where he stuck his collection of knives for cutting, slicing and chopping. Before plunging one into the meat the butcher would sharpen the blade on his steel, running it up and down, first one side then the other, against the metal rod. The sharp scraping noise set my teeth on edge to their very roots.

The rabbits were hung behind the glass pane, pink, quartered, their stomachs opened to reveal their fat livers – exhibitionists, crucified martyrs, sacrificial offerings to covetous housewives. The chickens were suspended by the neck, their skinny yellow necks stretched and pierced by the iron hooks which held their heads pointing skywards; fat bodies of poultry with grainy skin dangling wretchedly, with their whimsical parson's noses stuck above their arseholes like the false nose on a clown's face.

In the window, like so many precious objects, the different cuts of pork, beef and lamb were displayed to catch the eye of the customer. Fluctuating between pale pink and deep red, the joints caught the light like living jewels. Then there was the offal, the glorious offal, the most intimate, the most authentic, the most secretly evocative part of the deceased animal: flabby, dark, blood-red livers; huge, obscenely coarse tongues; chalky, enigmatic brains; kidneys coiled around their full girth, hearts tubed with veins – and those kept hidden in the fridge: the lights for granny's cat because they are too ugly; spongy grey lungs; sweetbread, because it is rare and saved for the best customers; and those goats' testicles, brought in specially from the abattoir and always presented ready wrapped, with the utmost discretion, to a certain stocky gentleman for his special treat.

About this unusual and regular order the boss and the butcher – who treated most things as an excuse for vulgar asides – never said a word.

As it happens I knew that the two men believed that the customer acquired and maintained an extraordinary sexual power through his weekly consumption of goats' testicles. In spite of the supposed benefits of this ritual they had never ventured to try it themselves. That part of the male anatomy, so often vaunted in all kinds of jokes and comments, nevertheless demanded respect. It went without saying that one could only go so far before trampling on sacred ground.

Those goat's testicles did not fail to excite my imagination. I had never managed to see them – had never dared ask. But I thought about that chubby pink packet and about the gentleman who carried it away without a word, after paying, like everyone else, at my till (the testicles were sold for some derisory sum). What was the taste and texture of these carnal relics? How were they prepared? And above all, what effect did they have? I too tended to attribute extraordinary properties to them, which I thought about endlessly.

He smiled, fixing his eyes on mine. This look was the signal. It penetrated behind my pupils, ran all over my body, thrust into my belly. The butcher was about to speak.

'How's my little darling this morning?'

Salivating like a spider spinning his web.

'Did she sleep well? Didn't find the night too long? Didn't miss anything?'

So it began. It was disgusting. And yet so sweet.

'Did you have someone round to take care of your little pussy? You like it, don't you? I can see it in your eyes. I was all alone, I couldn't get to sleep, I was thinking about you a lot, you know . . .'

The butcher completely naked, squeezing his penis in his hand. I felt sticky.

'I'd have preferred it if you were there, of course . . . But you'll come soon, my darling . . . You'll see how I'll take care of you . . . I've got skilful hands, you know . . . and a long tongue, you'll see. I'll lick your cunt like it's never been

licked. You can feel it already, can't you? Can
you smell the scent of love? Do you like the
smell of men when you're about to drink
them?'

He was breathing rather than speaking. His
words broke against my neck, trickled down
my back, over my breasts, my stomach, my
thighs. He held me with his small blue eyes,
his winning smile.

At this time the boss and the butcher-woman
were putting the finishing touches to their
display in the covered market, and giving last
minute orders to the staff; there were few
customers around as yet. As always when we
were alone together, the butcher and me, we
started the game, our game, our precious device
for annihilating the world. The butcher was
leaning on my till, right next to me. I did
nothing, I sat up straight on my high stool. I
listened, that's all.

And I knew that, in spite of myself, he could
see my desire rise beneath his words, he knew
the fascination his sweet-talking stratagem
exerted.

'I bet you're already wet inside those little
knickers of yours. Do you like me talking to you

like this? Do you like getting off on nothing but words ... I'd have to go on, forever ... If I touched you, you see, it would be like my words ... all over, gently, with my tongue ... I'd take you in my arms, I'd do whatever I want with you, you'd be my doll, my little darling to caress ... You would never want it to end ...'

The butcher was tall and fat, with very white skin. As he spoke without pause he breathed lightly, his voice grew husky and dissolved into a whisper. I saw his face fill with pink patches; his lips glistened with moisture; the blue of his eyes lightened until they were no more than pale luminous spots.

In my half-conscious state I wondered if he were not about to come, dragging me along with him, if we were not about to let our pleasure flow in this stream of words; and the world was white like his overall, like the window and like the milk of men and cows, like the fat belly of the butcher, under which was hidden the thing which made him talk, talk into my neck as soon as we were alone together, and young and hot like an island in the middle of the cold meat.

'What I like more than anything is eating the pussies of little girls like you. Will you let me, eh, will you let me graze on you? I'll pull open your pretty pink lips so softly, first the big ones, then the small ones, I'll put the tip of my tongue in, then the whole tongue, and I'll lick you from your hole to your button, oh your lovely button, I'll suck you my darling you'll get wet you'll shine and you'll never stop coming in my mouth just as you want eh I'll eat your arse and your breasts your shoulders your arms your navel and the small of your back your thighs your legs your knees your toes I'll sit you on my nose I'll smother myself in your mound your head on my balls my huge cock in your cute little mouth let me my darling I'll come in your throat on your belly or on your eyes if you prefer the nights are so long I'll take you from the front from behind my little pussy it'll never end never end . . .'

He was now whispering in my ear, leaning right over me without touching, and neither of us knew anything any more – where we were, where the world was. We were transfixed by a breath become speech which emerged on its own, had its own life, a disembodied animal, just between his mouth and my ear.

*

With his hand under the mincing machine, the butcher collected the meat which came out in long thin tubes, all squeezed together in a soft mass sinking down into the man's palm. The butcher switched off the machine and swallowed the red pile in two mouthfuls.

This afternoon I would write to Daniel.

Daniel. My true love, my dark angel. I would like to tell you I love you, and that my words should make a hole, a large hole in your body, in the world, in the dark mass of life. I would want this hole to attach you to me (I'd pass a strong rope through it like the ones which tie ships in harbour and which creak horribly in high winds), I would want this hole to dive into. To swim in your light, in your night of heavy velvet, in your flashes of silk. If only my words had the force of this love which makes a hole in my stomach and causes me pain. Strange, impossible enigma never to be resolved, exclamation mark which will always hold me upright in danger, standing on my head and racked with an overbearing dizziness.

Where are you, Daniel? My head is turning, the sea is singing, men are weeping and I am floating adrift on lakes of mercury; my hands before me, I recite old poems where the voices are too soft. Daniel Daniel . . . I love you do you hear? That means I want you, I throw you away, I abhor you, I'm empty of you, I'm full of you, I eat you, I swallow you, I take you whole, I destroy myself, I drive you into me, I stave myself in with you to death. And I kiss your eyelids and I suck your fingers, my love . . .

The butcher gave me a friendly wink. Had he forgotten everything already? He went to fetch a loin from the window, placed it on the stall and began cutting slices. He grabbed the chopper, opened the ribs already separated by the knife and with sharp strokes broke the vertebrae which held the meat together in a block.

'Does that suit madam?'

The butcher always displayed great politeness with his customers, paying them an emphatic compliment with his look, so long as they weren't too old or too ugly. Doubtless he would have loved to touch all those breasts and all those buttocks, manipulate them in his expert hands like so many cuts of meat. The butcher had flesh in his soul.

I watched him contemplating those bodies in their summer dresses with a scarcely disguised desire; and I saw him all hands and all sex, all fulfilment and desire. The fulfilment was the contact with cold meat, with death. But what kept the butcher alive was his desire, the constantly maintained demands of the flesh, given form every now and again in that breath between his mouth and my ear.

And little by little, by the magic of a power greater than my will, I felt his desire become my own. My desire contained at once the fat body of the butcher and all the others, those of the customers undressed by his eyes and even mine. An unending exasperation rose from my stomach at all this flesh.

'Little darling, you are so light next to me. I'll have to undress you with great care so as not to break you. You'll undress me too, first my shirt, then my trousers. I'll already have an erection, my cock is sure to be sticking out of my pants. You'll take them off next, you'll want to touch it straight away, to take that warm hard packet in your hands, you'll want its juice and you'll start to jerk it, to suck it and finally you'll put it between your legs, you'll stick yourself on my skewer and you'll gallop towards your pleasure until we both soak ourselves oh my darling I know it's been fermenting inside us for days it'll all explode we'll go wild we'll do things we've never done before and we'll ask for more and I'll give you my balls and my cock and you'll do whatever you want with them and you'll give me your cunt and your arse and I'll be the lord and master and I'll smear you with sperm and juice until your moon shines.'

Was it really the butcher's word which the breath carried? Daniel, why?

In the afternoon I would go back to my room at my parents' house. I would try to work on the painting which I had started at the beginning of the summer, but I would make no progress. I dreamed of the start of term, the time when this season would end, when I'd go back to my room in town, see my friends at art college, especially Daniel. I would pick up my paper, pens and ink and start to write to him, punctuating my letters with small drawings.

Most of the students at college liked to paint on huge canvases, often filling a whole wall. I wanted to compress the world, seize it and hold it whole in the smallest possible space. My works were miniatures to be seen up close, the details were the results of nights and nights of work. For some time I had wanted to move on to sculpture. My first attempts involved modelling balls of clay the thickness of a finger-nail; but after baking, my objects, hewn with a jeweller's precision, were no more than broken trinkets, crumbling at the first touch of my fingertips, leaving nothing but a trace of red powder on my skin.

And I read poetry, and in the evening I would recite to myself a passage from *Zarathustra* which dealt with the warm breath of the sea, its groans and its bad memories.

I had first met Daniel at my brother's place. They had just formed a rock group with that girl. She was sitting between them on the bed, her thin legs tightly clad in leopard-skin leg-gings and folded beneath her, her feet against her bottom. They were listening to music, talking about comic strips, laughing. Her large jumper showed off her rather heavy breasts. She bobbed her close-cropped head and made com-ments in a loud voice. She was the singer. Daniel looked at her a lot, and I fell in love with him immediately. At least, that's how it seemed, looking back at it.

I was smoking and drinking coffee like them

but I said nothing. They pressed close to her, laid a hand on her thigh every so often.

I wasn't listening. The cassette was very loud.

He was dark and his eyes darted like black-birds, landing on me momentarily and pecking me with their wicked beaks.

I had a pain in my stomach. I was lying on the ground. I hated that girl.

She had repulsive breasts, just like the Barbie doll I played with when I was small. He and my brother were obviously dying to touch them. Perhaps they already had. One hand each on her chest.

The air I was breathing descended in bitter shafts down to my navel.

I rolled over onto my stomach. I was smoking so much I felt my fingertips tingle. She folded and unfolded her legs, and her pants clung to her anatomy, to the little bulge between her legs with the split in the middle. I could feel the drumbeat hitting my thorax. I watched his eyes to see if he was also looking at that part of her body, below her jumper where her breasts bounced with each movement.

The bastard was looking.

*

The weather was getting hotter. It was the main topic of conversation. When the butcher came out of the freezer a customer would say, 'I bet it's nicer in there than out here?'

He would laugh in agreement. Sometimes, if he liked the woman, if she didn't look too unapproachable, he would hazard, 'Shall we try it then?' in as light a tone as possible, so as to distract attention from the glint in his eye.

His comment was not purely anodyne. It wasn't uncommon to see the boss and the butcher-woman come out of the freezer, ten minutes after going in, with buttons undone and hair dishevelled.

One day when the boss was away the butcher and the butcher-woman had locked themselves in the freezer. After a moment or two I had succumbed to the desire to open the door.

Between the rows of hanging carcasses of sheep and calves the butcher-woman was grabbing hold of two thick iron hooks above her head like someone keeping her balance on the tube or the bus. Her dress was pulled up and rolled around her waist exposing her thighs and her white stomach with her black tuft standing out in profile. The butcher was standing behind her, his trousers around his ankles, and his apron also twisted up around his belt, his flesh spilling out. They stopped fornicating when they saw me, but the butcher remained held in the butcher-woman's buxom behind.

Every time a customer mentioned the coolness of the freezer I saw that scene, the butcher-woman hanging like a carcass and the butcher pushing his excrescence into her in the middle of a forest of meat.

There was a constant flow of customers. The butcher no longer had time to talk. As he tossed the packets onto the scales he gave me winks, small signs.

As for the business with the butcher-woman, I had borne a grudge against him for several days, during which I had refused to let him whisper in my ear. So he began talking to me about his apprenticeship in the abattoirs. It was hard, very hard, it was a time he almost went mad, he told me. But he didn't take up the story, he quickly clammed up, his face clouded over.

Every day he brought up the abattoirs without being able to elaborate further. He became more and more gloomy.

Towards the end of the week, at half past one

in the afternoon (the worst time of day because of tiredness, the effect of the aperitif and the wait for lunch to be served), he got into an argument with one of the assistants who had just come back from the market. They were exchanging curt remarks in loud voices, their heads raised and their muscles taut. The assistant hurled some insult, and with a broad sweep of the hand, as if brushing his opponent aside, he went into the freezer. The butcher was livid with rage, I had never seen him like that before. He grabbed a large knife from the stall and, his eyes blazing with anger, leapt into the room after the assistant.

I dashed across, grabbed him by the left hand, calling him by his first name to stop him closing the door behind him.

That was the first time I had touched him. He turned to face me, hesitated for a moment, then followed me back into the shop.

After that I had let him start his whispering again. His descriptions of our hypothetical hours of love, originally fairly discreet, had become much more crude.

They rehearsed in the cellar of my block and on most occasions came up to see me. I had started wearing tight leatherette pants and jumpers squeezed over my little breasts, and enlarging the shape of my mouth with excessive lipstick.

She was there too, and I hesitated between the desire to please her, to like her and find her attractive, and the fierce jealousy she aroused in me. Sometimes I wanted to push her into Daniel's arms, to see him hold her round the waist, place his lips on hers — I imagined the scene in slow motion, the two faces leaning slowly towards each other, the soft impact of lips, the tongues foraging . . . But whenever I actually caught them exchanging a gesture of complicity, I felt like ripping out their mouths and eyes and smashing their heads together.

I offered them tea, and we chatted and smoked. When she wasn't wearing her leopard-skin pants she wore a short leather skirt and lace stockings, and always a black jacket and large extravagant earrings.

Daniel said one day that earrings were invented so that girls wouldn't discover the pleasure of having men nibble their earlobes. So she took off her earrings, sat herself on the knees of the two boys, who were sitting side by side, and had them bite both ears together as she cried out in a shrill voice, 'Oh yes, yes, I'm coming, I'm coming!' Then they laughed a lot, the three of them.

I watched them with curiosity and fear. Daniel was now living with my brother. The flat was quite large, and they shared the rent. I hardly ever went round there.

Daniel and my brother made fun of me because I locked myself away to paint these miniscule things. They adopted a protective tone with me, as if I were a little sister to both of them; they called me pretty when I tied my hair in a ponytail before working.

And I, wanting to die of love like in the old stories, starved myself of food, and each day before the mirror I admired the ever more prominent outline of my ribs, and the pallor which my weakness gave me. I had dizzy spells, my body felt light, I was transparent to the world.

In the afternoon I got into bed and cried into the pillow while thinking about Daniel, and in the end I took off my knickers to caress myself in my sweet sorrow, making myself come to the point of exhaustion.

When the man came into the shop I immediately lowered my eyes to avoid looking at him.

I pulled myself together, overcame my repulsion.

The man had no face left.

His head was no more than a huge ulcer, a formless mass covered with swellings, growths, extraordinary excrescences, disgusting boils protruding several centimetres from the pustulating surface, with a deep depression in the centre, veritable volcanoes of flesh.

I felt the blood drain from my extremities, black dots swam before my eyes, my stomach turned.

Globular head, human flesh, who knows whether you were beautiful? And you Siamese twins, dwarfs and giants, albinos, double-heads and cyclopses?

Who could ever understand the world? Its four-leafed clovers? Wasn't the world itself monstrous, weren't we its glorious rotting abscesses?

That morning I had thrown away a bunch of
roses which I had kept in my room for several
days. As soon as I had removed them from the
vase the foul smell of the water had filled the
room. The roses were still very beautiful. Their
slightly faded petals slipped from my hands and
spread across the floor in a pale coloured spray.
I picked them up one by one, incomparably soft
and delicate, and I felt the desire to relish them,
to weave them into a sensual dress, a pillow for
dreaming; when I had gathered a fistful, I
opened my hand and let it shed its petals over
the waste bin.

The man had left but his ghost remained.
The heat had become more intense. Out of
the bulb-head resting on the chopping block
bloomed a cluster of purulent diseases, blazing lesions, malignant affections. Hard purple
tongues, bloated ears, bodies exuding worms
from every pore; a woman removes a yellow
snake's head from her middle finger, pulls
gently on the creature extracting itself from
her arm, the worms writhe and seek to tear
themselves from the flesh, the stomach opens
and the putrid guts spill onto the ground like
a stream of mud, the seeds in the stomach
sprout foliage into the lungs, the heart glistens

the belly fills with water it is a deep sea where goldfish swim and catfish idle, where whales gurgle in oceans of milk to the song of the siren, and the squid, encumbered with arms, lurks in the depths of the waters behind its dark rock it is the genital cave where there are pink dolls with cruel faces this one has curls and smiles with two mouths she lies among the dancing algae and attracts sharks with her octopus-lips her belly is full of crabs and eyes of mad fish this other one flows and swells at the mercy of the currents its syrup-sweet waves carry pungent-scented bouquets and there she is erect her violet tip glistening from which bursts forth quite white the faded rose.

We were caught in a net of flesh like flies in a spider's web. I saw hanging still from the women's low-cut dresses and the men's shorts those lumps of soft matter from which they had scarcely managed to tear themselves in order to go out and about in the streets, on the beach, to resemble concrete, stone and sand, anything which has no throbbing blood, no beating heart, no swelling sex. Their meagre clothes, their pathetic suntans were not enough to disguise their shame. They still had to hide away to shit, piss and fuck.

That is why some people were so keen to maintain their bodies like machines, to shed all useless flesh – and they would rather have their meat well-dressed than their brains without muscle.

Customers, butcher's customers, bodies with dead souls! If you knew how much I hated you! With your perpetual taste for moderation, your holidaymakers' insouciance, the serious way you choose a piece of meat, the anxious way you look at the price on the scales, your condescending attitude towards the butcher and the cashier!

Unlike them you have never made up forbidden poems and uttered them in a low voice day after day.

The boss too spoke a secret language which you didn't understand. When he served you, madam, and said out loud and very quickly 'thar m'dam, 'sgot a lovely m'ttom that I'd lickab'm donicely', what could you reply? Perhaps you were aware of cracks appearing, perhaps you felt your poise totter a little. But you'd rather give nothing away, madam, because it would involve losing your honour, breaking your shell of ethereal majesty and above all having to cause a scandal and lose out on a nice leg of mutton, if you had cared to realise that the boss, your butcher, spoke a double language in public, standard speech and butcherese.

That night when we had come home late after the concert my brother had offered to put me up for the night.

I had tossed and turned for more than an hour in the little sofabed before getting up like a sleepwalker, going into Daniel's room and getting into bed next to him.

He had taken me in his arms, pressed me against his body, and I had felt his sex harden against my stomach.

He laughed at finding me there, naked in the middle of the night in his bed, and I felt my fear grow at the act to be performed, the man's body to be discovered. I wanted to love and I wanted Daniel, and I desperately clasped my skin to his skin, my heat to his heat, and he entered me twice and hurt me twice and ejaculated.

It was already morning. I left on foot. I was singing, laughing. I had not experienced the supreme pleasure, but I had been deflowered and I was madly in love.

I had got up in the dark and like a cat in the night I had walked down the dark corridor towards Daniel, my stomach churning, towards the warm man sleeping in the secrecy of his bed. And the two nocturnal creatures had recognised each other with ease, he had accepted me and taken me to him, I had touched his skin and sniffed his scent, he had put his sex in mine.

His sex in mine. At midday I still wanted it, but didn't dare to phone. Only that evening did I discover that Daniel had gone home to his family for the holidays.

When I had got home that morning I devoured three oranges, I remembered everything, I couldn't stop myself smiling. I didn't know yet that he had gone. I didn't know yet that he would go so often and return so seldom, that there would be so much waiting, so few nights and that I would never know the greatest pleasure.

I watched the butcher, and I desired him. He was ugly, granted, with his fat belly snug in his bloodstained apron. But his flesh was lovable.

Was it the late summer heat, the two months of separation from Daniel, or the butcher's words slobbered in my ear? I was in an almost intolerable state of excitement. The men who came into the shop I undressed with my eyes, I saw them become erect, I stuffed them between my legs. The women that the butcher and the boss desired, I raised their skirts, opened their legs and gave them to them. My head was full of obscene thoughts, my sex rose up in my throat, I wanted to relieve myself by hand behind the till, but that would not have been enough, not enough.

That afternoon I would go to the butcher's house.

Daniel, see how I am, panting and miserable. Put your hands on my head, Daniel, so that my anger might go, that my body might relax. Take me, Daniel, make me come.

Daniel. I tried to paint a bunch of roses. Don't laugh. How do you render the colour of a rose, its softness, its fineness, its delicacy, its scent? Nevertheless, I desire them, I attempt, I circle around.

Are we not stupid to want to capture the world with our pens and our brushes at the end of our right hands? The world does not know us, the world escapes us. I feel like crying when I see the sky, the sea, when I hear the waves, when I lie in the grass, when I look at a rose. I place my nose inside the rose and I suck the white of the grass, but the grass and the rose do not surrender themselves, the grass and the rose keep thcir terrible mystery.

Have you ever been struck by the mysterious presence of huge pumpkins in the middle of a kitchen garden? There they are, calm and luminous like Buddhas, as heavy as you are, and suddenly, before this strange creation of the earth, you are seized by doubt, you topple over outside of reality, you look at your own body in astonishment and you fumble around like a blind person. The garden remains impassive, it continues to hang its shiny tomatoes and peas in their pods, to cloak itself with sweet-smelling parsley and open-headed lettuce. And, quietly, you go away, a stranger.

Daniel. This afternoon, perhaps, I will go to the butcher's house. Don't be angry, I love only you. But the butcher is full of flesh and he has the soul of a child.

★

Daniel. This afternoon, probably, I will go to the butcher's house. It doesn't change anything, I love only you. But the butcher is depraved, I want him to stop dreaming about me.

You were worried, Daniel, when you saw me sitting on the window-sill on the third floor. You came up behind me without a sound, you grabbed me round the waist to scare me. We laughed, I swung my legs one last time into space, and you took me with you to the bed. It was when we were alone together. I hung my head backwards outside of the bed. I saw the whole room upside down, you sat on top of me, put your hands around my neck, softly you squeezed and the ceiling swam before my eyes.

Do you remember the day when we went to steal a boat from the beach, at dawn? I don't like stealing, the dawn was heartrending, I loved you.

If I go to the butcher's house it will be like killing us, Daniel. By laying his fat body on my body the butcher will kill your thin firm body. I loved your shoulders, broad and fine, covered in freckles. I loved your soft dark hair, your

thin mouth, your straight nose, your ears, your
eyes, I loved your voice, your laugh, I loved
your torso, your flat stomach, I loved your back
where my fingers wandered, I loved your smell
I didn't wash so as to keep it on me, I loved
going across town to meet you the streets said
it's this way he's at the other end the snow
glistened and the crowd parted to let me
through there was only me and the sun in the
sky both marching towards the magic cave
where love was waiting for me where I would
open my arms my coat and my legs where I
would undress you where you would stretch
out next to me skin to skin eye to eye mouth
to mouth where I would receive you for eter-
nity I loved waiting for you Daniel I loved your
sex which I have never been able to touch.

When the butcher is in my body Daniel we will
be dead our story will be dead and will become
the touchstone of my coming sorrows the
butcher with his sharpened blade the butcher
with his blade will cleave my belly and we will
depart from the belly where we were we will
have no more love enough in our hands to
touch each other again we will tear ourselves
apart and I will cry for you the butcher with his

blade will cleave and cleave again cleave and cleave again cleave and cleave again till he fills me with his white milk my eyes will bleed Daniel and my stomach will laugh and I will not write to you one last time you have abandoned me I will leave you because the moon stealer will never return to gather the stars there will be ghosts strangely similar to your sombre face they will come into my bed and I will soothe them we will give each other everything in the space of one night Daniel Daniel hear how my voice grows faint the butcher has thrown me completely naked on the stall he has raised his axe my head will roll on the bloody chopping block I will not see you again I will not hear you again he will lick me with his tongue so fresh he will eat me as he promised and there will be neither you nor me and I will be fine.

The temperature rose further. The butcher had become very serious and stared deep into my eyes whenever he turned round to the scales. Each time with a quickening pulse I inhaled the sickly breath of the meat.

I thought about my roses, whose water I had not changed, yet which remained so beautiful.

Of course, I had not succeeded in rendering their colour, like that of an old faded armchair cover, but partly transparent, a subtle shading off from pale pink to very pale brown on the edge of the petals.

I now let myself bathe in the warm air, rocked by the repetitive actions of work, the heavy gaze of the butcher. I was trapped in a passive waiting; time and things slid over me; there were glands in my body which were dead, whilst others fermented, driven by a secret purpose.

The people gave off a smell of sun oil and sea; the men still had sand stuck to the hair of their legs, the women on their necks and the bend of their elbows, the children had buckets and spades and vanilla ice-creams; the boss and the butcher moved busily between the window and the chopping block, the mincing machine and the freezer; the chopper cut the ribs with sharp hacks, the saw sawed the bone of the legs of mutton, the knives sliced the meat and I put the money in the till, soiled, well-thumbed notes.

Time passed and the butcher gave me a look which went right through my head. He was in the middle of cutting a side of meat with long black fibres when his hand slipped. His thumb began bleeding profusely, thick shiny red drops splattered onto the tiled floor. The butcher stuffed his finger into his apron, already stained with dark red streaks. He wanted to get back to work but the blood went on flowing out onto the chopping block.

When I came back the white cloth which I had placed under his hand was already soaked. I changed it. The drops of blood formed red flowers on the cloth. I opened the bottle of alcohol and poured it directly onto the finger. The butcher threw his head back, the wound sparkled. I wiped it gently, delicately placed the gauze bandage on the raw flesh and wound it slowly around the finger. The bandage turned red immediately; I wrapped it round again.

The mere smell of mown grass was enough to intoxicate me.

The thumb was now quite clean and clad in white like a bride. I felt the butcher looking at me. I found a thin rubber finger-stall and slid it over the bandaged thumb.

My eyes were lowered. I was in no hurry to let go of his hand.

*

In spite of the heat the butcher-woman had put the table outside in the shade of the trees. The boss, the butcher, and the market workers were drinking their second aperitif, and were indulging in slanging matches and laughter.

The butcher-woman brought out a dish of cold meats and a tomato salad. As she went past the boss laid his hand on one of her buttocks. She offered the other.

The butcher was sitting next to me. I served out his food because of his thumb. As usual, the boss was in a vulgar mood: 'I hear our little cashier's been tying ribbons round your digit.'

A sausage with a suggestively shaped end was the cause of further merriment.

The paté, potted meats, crackling and ham all disappeared in the blink of an eye.

The wine flowed, it was good stuff.

The butcher-woman brought out large steaks, as thick as your hand, and striped by the grill of the barbecue.

The boss and the butcher took a whole one each – the meat stuck out over the sides of their plates like dangling tongues. In spite of his injury the butcher cut his meat briskly into large pieces and gobbled them down. The laughter and the lewd remarks erupted continuously. I scarcely heard them; they were so familiar and I was in a wine-induced haze.

The heat was unbearable. There wasn't a breath of air, and the sky had turned to lead.

By the cheese course the excitement had reached its pitch. I vaguely heard a few gross obscenities. The butcher-woman was saying to one or other of the men gathered round the table: 'Go and wank yourself off, bring me a glassful and I'll drink it.'

A number of voices exclaimed: 'Bet you don't!'

Then the storm broke. Lightning, thunder and rain. A warm heavy tightly packed rain.

We cleared the table in a hurry, bumping into each other with cries and hearty laughter.

The plane trees began shaking their leaves.

II

Neither of us said a word. I watched the movement of the windscreen wipers. I grew sluggish with the smell of my wet hair next to my cheeks.

He opened the door, took me by the hand. My sandals were full of water, my feet squelched against the plastic soles. He led me to the lounge, sat me down, brought me a coffee. Then he turned on the radio and asked me to excuse him for five minutes. He had to take a shower.

I went over to the window, pulled the curtain open a little and watched the rain falling.

The rain made me want to piss. When I came out of the toilet I pushed open the bathroom door. The room was warm and all steamed up. I saw the broad silhouette through the shower curtain. I pulled it open a little and looked at him. He reached out a hand but I pulled away. I offered to scrub his back. I stepped onto the rim, put my hands under the warm water and picked up the soap, turning it over between my palms until I worked up a thick lather.

I began to rub his back, starting at the neck and shoulders, in circular movements. He was big and pale, firm and muscular. I worked my way down his spine, a hand on each side. I rubbed his sides, moving round a little onto his stomach. The soap made a fine scented froth, a cobweb of small white bubbles flowing over the wet skin, a slippery soft carpet between my palm and his back.

I went up and down the spine several times, from the small of the back to the base of the neck up to the first little hairs, the ones the barber shaves off for short haircuts with his deliciously vibrating razor.

I set off again from the shoulders and soaped each arm in turn. Although the limbs were relaxed, I felt bulging knots of muscle. His forearms were covered with dark hairs; I had to really wet the soap to make the lather stick. I worked back towards the deep hairy armpits.

I lathered up my hands again and massaged his buttocks in a revolving motion. Though on the big side, his buttocks had a harmonious shape, curving gracefully from the small of the back and joining the lower limbs without flab.

I went over and over their roundness to know their form with my palms as well as with my eyes. Then I moved down the hard solid legs. The hairy skin covered barriers of muscle. I felt I was penetrating a new, wilder region of the body down to the strange treasure of the ankles.

Then he turned towards me. I raised my head and saw his swelling balls, his taut cock, straight above my eyes.

I got up. He didn't move. I took the soap between my hands again and began to clean his broad, solid, moderately hairy chest.

I began to move slowly down over his distended stomach, surrounded by powerful abdominal muscles. It took some time to cover the whole surface. His navel stood out, a small white ball outlined by the rounded mass, a star around which my fingers gravitated, straining to delay the moment when they would succumb to the downward pull towards the comet erected against the harmonious round form of the stomach.

I knelt down to massage his abdomen. I skirted round the genital area slowly, quite gently, towards the inside of the thighs.

His penis was incredibly large and erect.

I resisted the temptation to touch it, continuing to stroke over the pubis and between the legs. He was now lying back against the wall, his arms spread, with both hands pressed against the tiles, his stomach jutting forward. He was groaning.

I felt he was going to come before I even touched him.

I moved away, sat down fully under the shower spray, and with my eyes still fixed on his over-extended penis, I waited until he calmed down a little.

The warm water ran over my hair, inside my dress. Filled with steam, the air frothed around us, effacing all shapes and sounds.

He had been at the peak of excitement, and yet had made no move to hasten the denouement. He was waiting for me. He would wait as long as I wanted to make the pleasure last, and the pain.

I knelt down in front of him again. His cock, already thickly inflated, sprang up.

I moved my hand over his balls, back up to their base near the anus. His cock stood up again, more violently. I held it in my other hand, squeezed it, began slowly pulling it up and down. The soapy water I was lathered with

46

provided perfect lubrication. My hands were filled with a warm, living, magical substance. I felt it beating like the heart of a bird, I helped it ride to its deliverance. Up, down, always the same movement, always the same rhythm, and the moans above my head. And I was moaning too, with the water from the shower sticking my dress to me like a tight silken glove, with the world stopped at the level of my eyes, of his belly, at the sound of the water trickling over us and of his cock sliding under my fingers, at the warm and tender and hard things between my hands, at the smell of the soap, of the soaking flesh and of the sperm mounting under my palm.

The liquid spurted out in bursts, splashing my face and my dress.

He knelt down as well, and licked the tears of sperm from my face. He washed me the way a cat grooms itself, with diligence and tenderness.

His plump white hand, his pink tongue on my cheek, his washed-out blue eyes, the eyelids still heavy as if under the effect of a drug. And his languid heavy body, his body of plenitude . . .

A green tender field of showers in the soft breeze of the branches ... It is autumn, it is raining, I am a little girl, I am walking in the park and my head is swimming because of the smells, of the water on my skin and my clothes, I see a fat man over there on the bench looking at me so intently that I pee myself, standing up, I am walking and I am peeing myself, it is my warm rain on the park, on the ground, in my knickers, I rain, I give pleasure ...

He took off my dress, slowly.

Then he stretched me out on the warm tiles and, with the shower still running, began planting kisses all over my body. His powerful hands lifted me up and turned me over with extreme delicacy. Neither the hardness of the floor nor the pressure of his fingers could bruise me.

I relaxed completely. And he placed the pulp of his lips, the wetness of his tongue in the hollow of my arms, under my breasts, on my neck, behind my knees, between my buttocks, he put his mouth all over, the length of my back, the inside of my legs, right to the roots of my hair.

He lay me on my back on the ground, on the

warm slippery tiles, lifted my hips with both hands, his fingers firmly thrust into the hollow as far as the spine, his thumbs on my stomach. He placed my legs over his shoulders and brought his tongue up to my vulva. I arched my back sharply. Thousands of drops of water from the shower hit me softly on my stomach and on my breasts. He licked me from my vagina to my clitoris, regularly, his mouth stuck to my outer lips. My sex became a channelled surface from which pleasure streamed, the world disappeared, I was no more than this raw flesh where soon gigantic cascades splashed, in sequence, continually, one after the other, forever.

Finally the tension slackened, my buttocks fell back onto his arms, I recovered gradually, felt the water on my stomach, saw the shower once more, and him, and me.

He had dried me off, put me in the warm bed, and I had fallen asleep.

I woke up slowly to the sound of the rain against the tiles. The sheets and pillow were warm and soft. I opened my eyes. He was lying next to me, looking at me. I placed my hand on his sex. He wanted me again.

I wanted nothing else but that. To make love, all the time, without rage, with patience, persistence, methodically. Go on to the end. He was like a mountain I must climb to the summit, like in my dreams, my nightmares. It would have been best to emasculate him straight away, to eat this still hard still erect still demanding piece of flesh, to swallow it and keep it in my belly, for ever more.

I drew close, raised myself a little, put my arms around him. He took my head between his hands, led my mouth to his, thrust his tongue in all at once, wiggled it at the back of my throat, wrapped it and rolled it over mine. I began biting his lips till I tasted blood.

Then I mounted on top of him, pressed my vulva against his sex, rubbed it against his balls and his cock. I guided it by hand and pushed it into me and it was like a giant flash, the dazzling entry of the saviour, the instantaneous return of grace.

I raised my knees, bent my legs around him and rode him vigorously. Each time when at the crest of the wave I saw his cock emerge glistening and red I held it again and tried to push it even further in.

I was going too fast. He calmed me down gently. I unfolded my legs and lay on top of him. I lay motionless for a moment, contracting the muscles of my vagina around his member.

I chewed him over the expanse of his chest; an electric charge flowed through my tongue, my gums. I rubbed my nose against the fat of his white meat, inhaled its smell, trembling. I was squinting with pleasure. The world was no more than a vibrant abstract painting, a clash of marks the colour of flesh, a well of soft matter I was sinking into with the joyous impulse of perdition. A vibration coming from my eardrums took over my head, my eyes closed. An extraordinarily sharp awareness spread with the waves surging through my skull, it was like a flame, and my brain climaxed, alone and silent, magnificently alone.

He rolled over onto me, and rode me in turn, leaning on his hands so as not to crush me. His balls rubbed against my buttocks, at the entry to my vagina, his hard cock filled me, slid and slid along my deep walls, I dug my nails into his buttocks, he breathed more heavily . . . We came together, on and on, our fluids mingled, our groans mingled, coming from further than

the throat, the depths of our chests, sounds
alien to the human voice.

It was raining. Enveloped in a large T-shirt
which he had lent me I was leaning on the
window-sill, kneeling on the chair placed
against the wall.

If I knew the language of the rain, of course, I
would write it down, but everyone recognises
it, and is able to recall it to their memory. Being
in a closed space while outside all is water,
trickling, drowning . . . Making love in the
cramped backseat of a car, while the windows
and roof resonate with the monotonous rain-
drops . . . The rain undoes bodies, makes them
full of softness and damp patches . . . slimy and
slobbering like snails . . .

He was also wearing a T-shirt, lying on the
couch, his big buttocks, his big genitals, and
his big legs bare.

He came over to me and pressed his hard
cock against my buttocks. I wanted to turn
round but he grabbed me by the hair, pulled my
head back and began to push himself into my
anus. It hurt, and I was trapped on the chair,
condemned to keep my head pointing
skywards.

Finally he entered fully, and the pain sub-sided. He began to move up and down, I was full of him, I could feel nothing except his huge monster cock right inside, whilst outside the bucketing rain poured down pure liquid light.

Continuing to jerk himself in me, to dig at me like a navvy while keeping my head held back, he slid two fingers into my vagina, then pulled them out. So I put in my own and felt the hard cock pounding behind the lining, and I began to fondle myself to the same rhythm. He speeded up his thrusts, my excitement grew, a mixture of pain and pleasure. His stomach bumped against my back with each thrust of the hips, and he penetrated me a bit further, invaded me a bit further. I wanted to free my head but he pulled my hair even harder, my throat was horribly stretched, my eyes were turned stubbornly towards the emp-tying sky, and he struck me and hammered me to the depths of myself, he shook up my body and then filled me with his hot liquid which came out in spurts, striking me softly, pleasurably.

A large drop would regularly drip somewhere with the sound of hollow metal. He let go of my hair, I let my head sink against the casement and began to sway imperceptibly.

I had him undress and stretch out on his back on the ground. With the expanders on his exercise machine I tied his arms to the foot of the bed, his legs to those of the table.

We were both tired. I sat down in the armchair and looked at him for a moment, spread-eagled and motionless.

His body pleased me like that, full of exposed imprisoned flesh, burst open in its splendid imperfection. Uprooted man, once more pinned to the ground, his sex like a fragile pivot exiled from the shadows and exposed to the light of my eyes.

Everything would have to be a sex; the curtains, the moquette, the expanders and the furniture, I would need a sex instead of my head, another instead of his.

We would both need to be hanging from an iron hook face to face in a red fridge, hooked by the top of the skull or the ankles, head down, legs spread, our flesh face to face, rendered powerless to the knife of our sexes burning like red-hot irons, brandished, open. We would need to scream ourselves to death under the tyranny of our sexes, what are our sexes?

Last summer, first acid, I lost my hands first of all, and then my name, the name of my race, lost humanity from my memory, from the knowledge of my head and of my body, lost the idea of man, of woman, or even of creature; I sought for a while, who am I? My sex. My sex remained to the world, with its desire to piss. The only place where my soul had found refuge, had become concentrated, the only place where I existed, like an atom, wandering between sky and grass, between green and blue, with no other feeling than that of a pure atom-sex, just, barely, driven by the desire to piss, gone astray, blissful, in the light, Saint-Laurent peninsula, it was one summer's day, no it was autumn, it took me all night and the next morning to come down, but for months afterwards when I pissed I lost myself, the moment of dizziness that's it, I draw myself back entirely into my sex as if into a navel, my being is there in that sensation in the centre of the body, the rest of the body annihilated, I no longer know myself, have no form nor title, the ultimate trip each time and sometimes still, just an instant, like being hung head down in the great spiral of the universe, but only you know what those moments mean, afterwards I say to myself 'is that really who I am?' and 'how beautiful the world is, with all those bunches of black grapes, how good it is to go grape-picking at the height of summer, with the sun catching the grapes and the eyes of the pickers, the vines are twisted, how I'd love to piss at the end of the row!', and there are all sorts of stupid things like that in our bodies, so good do we feel after that weird dizziness which we miss a little, nevertheless, already.

I got up, knelt with my legs apart above his head. Still out of range of his face, I pulled open my outer lips with my fingers and gave him a long look at my vulva.

Then I stroked it slowly, with a rotating movement, from my anus to my clitoris.

I would have wanted grey skies where hope is focused, where quivering trees spread their fairy arms, capricious, hot-headed dreams in the grass kissed by the wind, I would have wanted to feel between my legs the huge breath of the millions of men on earth. I would have wanted, look, look at what I want . . .

I pushed the fingers of my left hand into my vagina, continued to rub myself. My fingers are not my fingers, but a heavy ingot, a thick square ingot stuck inside me, dazzling with gold to the dark depths of my dream. My hands went faster and faster. I rode the air in spasms, threw my head back, weeping onto his eyes as I came.

I regained the armchair. His face had turned red, he grew erect again, fairly softly. He was defenceless.

When I was small, I knew nothing about love. Making love, that magic word, the promise of that unbelievably wonderful thing which would happen all the time as soon as we were big. I had no idea about penetration, not even about what men have between their legs, in spite of all those showers with my brothers. You can look and look in vain, what do you know, when you have the taste for mystery?

When I was even smaller, no more than four, they talked in front of me thinking that I wasn't listening; Daddy told about a madman who ran screaming through the woods at night. I open the gate of my grandmother's garden, and all alone with my alsatian bitch I enter the woods. At the first gap in the trees, on a mound of sand, I lie down with the bitch, up against her warm flank, an arm around her neck. She puts out her tongue and she waits, like me. No one. The pines draw together and bend over us, in a tender, scary gesture. In the middle of the woods there is a long concrete drain, bordered with brambles where blackberries grow, and where one day a kart driver, hurtled violently off the track in front of me and put his eyes out. There is a blockhouse with a black mouth disguised as a door, and right at the end a washing plant devoured by moss and grass. Preserved in the watercourse is the hardened print of an enormous foot.

I went and lay on the ground next to him, laid my head on his stomach, my mouth against his cock, one hand on his balls, and I went to sleep. Certainly the footprint in the wet cement was of a big, strong, blond and probably handsome soldier.

When I woke up next to his penis I took it in my mouth, sucked it in several times with my tongue, felt it swell and touch the back of my throat. I massaged his balls, licked them, then returned to his cock. I placed it in the hollow of both my eyes, on my forehead, on my cheeks, against my nose, on my mouth, my chin, my throat, put my neck on it, squeezed it between my shoulder blades and my bent head, in my armpit, then the other, brushed against it with my breasts till I almost reached a climax, rubbed it with my stomach, my back, my buttocks, my thighs, squeezed it between my arms and my folded legs, pressed the sole of my foot against it, until I had left a trace of it over the whole of my body.

Then I put it back in my mouth and gave it a long suck, like you suck your thumb, your mother's breast, life, while he moaned and panted, always, until he ejaculates, in a sharp lamentation, and I drink his sperm, his sap, his gift.

I insisted on putting on my wet dress and going back on foot. The rain had stopped.

Without intending to I arrived at the beach. The sea was high and strong, the sand was wet, there was no one about. I went down to the water. It was dark and heavy with grey surf. I wandered along the shoreline in a zigzag – as the waves ebbed and flowed, bringing in millions of little bubbles, like soap lather.

The dunes had the forms and colours of flesh. I pushed my two fingers into the soft wet mass. The sea never stopped oozing, rubbing itself incessantly against the sand, chasing after its pleasure.

Where is love, if not in the burning pain of desire, jealousy, separation?

Daniel will never lie next to my body. Daniel is dead, I buried him behind the dune. His body which I will love no more, the body which the butcher's knife sliced and separated from mine. Ghost which goes on loving far from me, ghost,

my belly is gaping. I made your sex with my
two fingers to fuck the earth, that slut, who
won't love me, me the man, me the woman,
flesh and blood, stomach torn by childbirth,
mortal meat to inhabit.

I went up to the foot of a dune, sat down in the
sand, dry and tender like my bones. Soft slope
of time.

I was taken to the Black Cat by four boys I had
just met at the Beach Bar where I had gone to
get warm. In the back seat of the car Pierre and
Dominique held me by the shoulders, kissed
me on the cheek and laughed.

It was a 'masked ball', and the club was
overrun by a forest of rigid, grimacing, gro-
tesque faces. I danced with many different
partners, only able to appreciate them by their
bodies. As they couldn't kiss, the couples
touched each other a lot, blindly.

When a slow number came on Pierre asked
me to dance. He was eighteen years old, he had
long legs and, underneath his rubber death's
head, a sweet little nose. I pressed my head
hard against his chest, my hands on his back,
and I let him caress me.

When the song ended he took me by the hand, removed his mask and led me outside.

It was a cool night, a starless sky. Pierre drew me towards him, I held him tight with pleasure. He kissed me.

In the car he kissed me again. Then he switched on his headlights, started the engine.

He pulled up on the road through the forest. He began kissing me again.

He helped me out, and, holding me by the neck, went with me into the wood.

He made me stretch out on the ground and lay on top of me, lifting up my dress. I had nothing on underneath, and I realised he had dropped his trousers. It was pitch black, I couldn't see a thing. Pierre entered me immediately, and soon began puffing noisily. I strained my eyes into the darkness, tried to distinguish the sky from the trees. Soon I saw a lighter patch, and something moving in it. Suddenly the moon emerged from the cloud and threw a milky light over us.

Then I saw the death's head above me.

I let out a cry, and the boy cried out also as his sperm shot into my belly.

Dawn found me lying in the ditch. I was sticky, full of earth, thirsty, lying in a hole which in winter served as a drain.

Day was breaking, killing off the shadows with their retinue of mysteries. And the light was even more disturbing, it forced you to see everything, know everything. Nevertheless, I welcomed it with a smile.

The birds of the daytime had all started singing together. I was going to go home and paint.

When I tried to get out of the hole I found that I couldn't move. My right arm was paralysed from my shoulder to my hand. With the slightest movemet painful twinges ran up my back and legs.

All night long I had heard the sea dreaming on hard pillows and the quivering forest. I had run in the shadows and had bumped into trees with sharp roots, I had cried black tears and I had fallen into the ditch, into the warm earth which had received me, I had slept in the hollow of the bed of earth, beneath the huge layer of coal, beneath the crow's wing, in the obscure hooting of the owls.

The vibrant scintillating night had passed over me, I had drunk it in large mouthfuls, and I was full of it.

And now the day was breaking and tearing up the shadows, which now hung in tatters beneath the trees. And then came the first ray of sun, which crossed the road and shot through the branches like the sharp line of a blade. And the whole of the night was erased.

The cries of the birds grew louder. In the grass, beneath the pine needles, things began scuttling around. I heard the sea, still, now no doubt mottled with light.

A car passed.

I tried to get up again. I was sore all over, but I made the effort to drag myself up by pushing on my left elbow. I scarcely moved, I remained immobilised by the pain. I tried again, managed a few centimetres.

At this spot the ditch was too deep for me to consider climbing out in my present state. I would have to move along until I found a gentler gradient.

I began crawling along on my left elbow

without stopping, in spite of the piercing pain which accompanied the slightest movement. I covered ground in miniscule steps, miniature steps which I could have included in my paintings. I laughed as I thought about Daniel, our bungled lovemaking, his shoddy sanity.

I laughed without a voice, with painful spasms in my sides and back at each jolt. But I was happy and I laughed again, my head next to the pine needles.

I crawled onwards, throwing my elbow in front of my head, digging it into the ground and dragging the rest of my body behind it. The pains subsided gradually and I was soon able to use my knees.

I liked this ditch, I was happy dragging myself along in it. It was a beautiful ditch, with grass and dew, and black loamy earth, and a carpet of pine needles, beneath which lived a world of tiny creatures.

A few metres ahead of me the ditch widened out, opened into a basin. It was the way out I had been expecting. I redoubled my efforts.

I reached the spot where the slope was less steep. My right arm was still virtually useless. I started the climb using my left forearm, the tips of my toes and my knees. I slid back down several times and was forced to start all over again. But I didn't give up until I reached the top.

When I reached the roadside the sense of my own tenacity made me breathe great lungfuls of air. I managed to get up on all-fours.

I found I was getting some response from my right arm. My dress was all torn, I felt the traces of sperm running down the inside of my thighs, the skin of my limbs, scratched and rubbed raw, was smarting.

I was by the roadside. I began to make my way on-all-fours.

You never realise how many things you can find by the roadside: numerous types of grass, flowers, mushrooms, all different pebbles and all sorts of tiny creatures . . .

I heard a car coming some way off. I lay as flat as I could on the ground. With every chameleon bone in my body I became grass, roadside.

The car went past.

The road stretched dead straight in front of me. I only had a few kilometres to go, and I could walk on-all-fours now. My heart filled with joy.

Luckily there was no one about. If anyone had seen me there they would have taken pity on me and spoiled my happiness full of hope.

People are like that: they can't see how beautiful your life is, they think your life must be terribly sad if, for example, it is mid-summer and you don't have a tan. They want you to agree with them where true joy is to be found, and if you are weak enough to go along with this you will never again have the chance to sleep alone in a ditch in the black night.

Down on-all-fours I imagined I was a dog, a cat, an elephant, a whale. The sun was rising in front of me, warming my face which was streaming with sweat. Whales have oceans to live in, they spout water to dampen their faces. I grazed on a little grass to refresh myself. Accidentally I also ate a few insects who happened to be passing.

Soon I felt strong enough to try standing up. With my hands still on the ground I unstuck my knees from the earth and lifted my rump. When I felt the firm ground under my feet I let my hands go and, as if on a bike, threw myself backwards, taking care to counterbalance the swing so as not to fall over.

I started walking, barefoot on the roadside, on the grass and the pebbles, and all those things you wouldn't realise were there.

*

Cars went past. One stopped but I didn't want to get in. I was more solid than ever. I had the strength of the butcher and the cunning of a boy with the death's head.

A broad avenue opened before me. I was going to paint a boat and when the rain returned I would be ready. I would take on board the animals of the earth and a butcher, and we would sail together till the end of the flood.

I reached the first house, surrounded by a hedge abundant in roses. I cut one, pulled off its petals in clumps and ate them. Their fineness and delicacy were in vain, I stuffed my mouth with them. The guard dog ran up to the gate, barking and growling with bared teeth. I finished eating the flower, and threw him the thorny stem.

A Selected List of Titles Available from Minerva

While every effort is made to keep prices low, it is sometimes necessary to increase prices at short notice. Mandarin Paperbacks reserves the right to show new retail prices on covers which may differ from those previously advertised in the text or elsewhere.

The prices shown below were correct at the time of going to press.

☐	7493 9137 5	**On the Eve of Uncertain Tomorrows**	Neil Bissoondath	£5.99
☐	7493 9050 6	**Women In A River Landscape**	Heinrich Boll	£4.99
☐	7493 9921 X	**An Instant in the Wind**	Andre Brink	£5.99
☐	7493 9147 2	**Explosion in a Cathedral**	Alejo Carpentier	£5.99
☐	7493 9109 X	**Bodies of Water**	Michelle Cliff	£4.99
☐	7493 9060 3	**Century of the Wind**	Eduardo Galeano	£4.99
☐	7493 9080 8	**Balzacs Horse**	Gert Hofmann	£4.99
☐	7493 9093 X	**The Notebook**	Agota Kristof	£4.99
☐	7493 9174 X	**The Mirror Maker**	Primo Levi	£4.99
☐	7493 9143 X	**Parents Worry**	Gerard Reve	£4.99
☐	7493 9172 3	**Lives of the Saints**	Nino Ricci	£4.99
☐	7493 9003 4	**The Fall of the Imam**	Nawal El Saadawi	£4.99
☐	7493 9924 4	**Ake**	Wole Soyinka	£5.99
☐	7493 9139 1	**The Four Wise Men**	Michel Tournier	£5.99
☐	7493 9092 1	**Woman's Decameron**	Julia Voznesenskaya	£5.99

All these books are available at your bookshop or newsagent, or can be ordered direct from the publisher. Just tick the titles you want and fill in the form below.

Mandarin Paperbacks, Cash Sales Department, PO Box 11, Falmouth, Cornwall TR10 9EN.

Please send cheque or postal order, no currency, for purchase price quoted and allow the following for postage and packing:

UK including BFPO — £1.00 for the first book, 50p for the second and 30p for each additional book ordered to a maximum charge of £3.00.

Overseas including Eire — £2 for the first book, £1.00 for the second and 50p for each additional book thereafter.

NAME (Block letters) ....

ADDRESS ....

....

☐ I enclose my remittance for ....

☐ I wish to pay by Access/Visa Card Number ⬚⬚⬚⬚⬚⬚⬚⬚⬚⬚⬚⬚⬚⬚⬚⬚

Expiry Date ⬚⬚⬚⬚